Jastine

Ecta: The Divide

I Love You lots
Samantha
Hanginton

Kyle Perkins

&

Samantha Harrington

Dedication

I dedicate this book to my Street Team; My Harem.

~Kyle Perkins

To Virginia, thanks for making this book happen, you really are one in a million.

To Kyle, you really did make writing this book together fun and I look forward to more in the future.

To my kids, never stop believing in yourself.

~Samantha Harrington

Ecta: The Divide

Editing

Virginia Johnson

and

Samantha Smith

Ecta: The Divide

Chapter One

When you live in SkyWaard long enough, you begin to notice the cracks in the ship. Now, I'm not saying that there are actual cracks, or any ship for that matter. No, these are cracks you cannot see. The kind that form underneath the skin of every man, locked away tightly in isolation. I'm a victim, too! Just another unfortunate soul aboard the zeppelins.

You, though... you have a choice. You don't have to be here, so why do you even bother? Sure, steel doors are strong, but what about your own resolve, man?! Will you just be another husk wandering through the prison that is your life, or will you choose to take the plunge? It's not like I am prompting you to do something you don't want to do.

You have thought of this very moment your entire life, and now... look at you. Your legs are failing you. Your courage is failing you. Worst of all, it's your own silly upbringing that is guarding your cell, keeping you from leaving. So what will it be, my boy? Are we seeing the makings of a coward, or is this just a comical story that you will tell your friends once you are a legend?

I've always held mirrors in contempt, as they seem to point out my flaws on a grand scale. Don't get me wrong, women find me quite attractive, but they aren't as attuned to the glaring imperfections that I see when I survey my own reflection. Where they see a tall, well-built, handsome man, I see a little boy trapped by my own mind.

It's partially my fault, I don't let anyone close enough to see these insecurities that I have strategically plastered over with my charming smile and no small amount of bravado. It is all simply a smoke screen; all a beautiful diversion from the problem areas I choose to ignore. That is, until they are staring me back in the face; it is then that I cannot ignore them.

Life has not been so incredibly easy for me, contrary to popular belief in this ward. It is true that I have always had a luxurious roof over my head, tailored suits on my back, and fine things at my disposal... but the isolation that wealth introduces to a man's life is unfathomable to those who haven't experienced it. For most, I am seen as simply ungrateful, and perhaps I am to some degree. What am I supposed to feel like, though? Society has this idea of what brings happiness, but they truly have no clue until they have lived on both sides of the aisle.

I have. I have seen both sides, and the sense of community that people have in the lesser wards is unrivaled. Once you achieve the wealth that my family has, your entire existence revolves around maintaining it, not the relationships with the people around you. People become a commodity, like anything else.

That is why I have chosen to give it all up. Simply walk away at the first opportunity.

The grand council sent out fliers across our network of zeppelins, informing the people that adventure awaited them on the ground. It was almost as they were speaking to me directly, right to my very soul. They have not yet said what this adventure is, or why they couldn't just send their own soldiers. Part of me wonders if it is because they do not wish to be implicated in some nefarious plan that they have concocted. Either way, today, I will be seeing what all the fuss is about. I am set to meet them in their zeppelin at noon.

I would like to pretend I am above the feelings of excitement that build inside of me at the thought of meeting the council, but alas, I am just a man. Anyone in SkyWaard would be honored.

They have been the sequestered central anchor to the fleet. Off-limits to all except those who receive special invitation. So, I suppose you could call me special. At least for today.

I shake my head rapidly, trying to clear the thoughts racing in my mind and I walk out into the main living area of my home. The place is a mess, pillows and blankets along with various women's undergarments decorate the living area. The bronze-colored walls are marked up with stains from Champaign splashes, earned in the soiree last night, no doubt. From the looks of the three naked women in front of me, it seems it was a night to remember – not that I do. My head is pounding, which is pretty par for the course on a weekday.

I walk over to one of the ladies and gently nudge her with my foot. "Come now, to your feet," I say in my most indifferent tone.

The woman's eyelids flicker open, revealing a pair of sleepy blue eyes. She rapidly sits up, "Oh no! What time is it?"

"It is time to show off your house keeping skills, my dear," I say with a grin.

My smile has always seemed to do the trick, women become my thralls once my dimples make their first appearance. If that doesn't work, my bright blue eyes or athletic physique usually seals the deal.

"Oh, right. Sorry for the mess," she looks around the room, then attempts to nudge her two friends awake.

"Cassandra, correct? I am terrible with names," I smile apologetically to the curvy woman.

"She's Cassandra, I'm Angelica," she replies, pointing to her friend as a look of disappointment washes over her own features.

"My apologies. Last night was a blur for me, as I'm sure it was for you. Please don't fault me for my spotty memory," I say, flashing another smile, hoping to be forgiven.

Angelica smiles back as she climbs up to her knees with the grace of a toddler learning to walk. "Instead of housekeeping, maybe I could show you other areas I excel in?" she asks suggestively as she creeps over to me and begins rubbing the front of my trousers. I can feel myself getting hard at the slightest provocation of her touch, but if I don't get out of here quickly, I may be late for my meeting with the council.

"So what do you say, Sebastian? You up for a little fun?" she purrs, looking up at me with her big blue eyes while licking her perfect lips.

At this point, I *could* resist her. I could tell her that it was a very lovely evening, but she should probably head home. You know, be responsible. However, I already know that is not how this will play out. Hopefully the council will accept a sincere apology?

Angelica takes off her shirt in front of me, revealing a set of perfect, perky tits, just as her friends stumble out of the front door.

The least they could have done is helped their friend, here. It is simply rude to leave her with this full work load.

She is absolutely beautiful as she sits on her knees with her eyes pleading to me. Her hair falls down across her chest when she pulls out the brass clip that was pinning it in place. She is ready for business.

"Alright, but after this, you must go. I have a very important meeting to attend and I cannot be late. No time for fun and games, you have to make this quick," I say in my best attempt to sound stern.

"Yes, of course, love. Don't worry, this won't take long," she says as she slides down my trousers and a look of genuine surprise crosses her face.

I could have sworn we did this last night, but perhaps it was one of the other two. Impossible to tell, really. All I have in my mind is clips from a montage of various sex positions from the night before. Maybe it will come back to me, maybe not. It's usually how my weekdays go.

Angelica brings her mouth right to the underside of my cock, I can feel her warm breath against it as she slowly drags her tongue from the base to the tip. The sensation hits me all at once and the feeling is dizzying.

I realize standing may not be the best idea during a hangover.

I grab her hand and lead her over to a chair in the corner of the room. As we arrive at our destination, she brings her hand up to my chest and assists me in taking a seat. A light suggestion to relax, I suppose.

I feel her tongue dance across my cock and I lean my head back in the chair, staring at the intricate carvings in the metal on the ceiling.

Angelica rises up higher so that her tits are resting on my knees and she leans over me to get a deeper angle. I feel her full lips slide over the head and her tongue guides me back into her throat. The sensation sends shockwaves through my body. I relish the warmth of her mouth as she begins sliding my cock in and out.

I decide to help her out, grabbing a handful of that pretty golden hair that she let down just for this occasion. As she picks up speed, with her moaning sending shockwaves through me, I begin pushing her head down onto it further. I thrust upward into her throat, watching her eyes tear up. She looks up to me and forces a smile.

Poor girl is trying to impress me, least I could do is give her a proper fuck.

I use her hair to lift her head up, forcing my cock out of her mouth as she slides her tongue up the front in one last attempt to make an impression with her mouth. I stand up from my chair with her still on her knees, keeping my hand on the back of her head. I won't allow her to get any ideas about switching positions.

Once I am behind her, I release her hair and move my hand down her back until I reach her skirt. I lift the fabric and let it fall onto her back, revealing a perfectly round ass, so beautiful I am tempted to bite it.

"You're going to be late," she says with a muffled snicker into the cushion of the chair.

"You're going to be sore," I fire back as I slide my cock slowly inside of her to the sound of a gasp; I'm unsure if it was hers or mine.

11

Her pussy is so tight it feels like it's cutting off the circulation to the head of my dick. I feel every single fold and ridge inside her as I continue to thrust deeper and deeper.

Her moans begin to pick up in intensity as I pick up my pace. I watch her ass jiggle against my skin as I thrust into her harder. Watching her beautiful ass move to the rhythm of my fucking... it is fucking amazing. Her soft moans tell me a story about my performance that she likely wouldn't have the words for.

I reach around her thigh and begin rubbing her clit with two fingers as I lean my chest against her back. She lets out a new type of moan as my fingers work their magic. She seems to be responding well to the old "Sebastian charm."

I watch as her fingers cling to the chair cushion and I feel her pussy contract around me in waves. With every flutter I watch her knuckles go white. I move my free hand over to her wide hips and begin pulling her into me. Moans stop midway as her breath is knocked out by the force of my plunges.

She looks back at me, almost in disbelief, as if she didn't think I had it in me. Her big beautiful eyes take me off of my rhythm for a moment, stopping me in my tracks. I can feel the urge to cum building inside of me as my breath begins to run ragged.

I force myself to concentrate. I pick up speed with my fingers as I feel her clit become unstable. It starts twitching with every swipe of my hand and I feel her body begin to tighten up.

"Se- Sebastian..." she moans out loud as her back arches and she throws her head back.

I feel her contract and contort wildly around my cock as every muscle in her body tenses up. I move my hand from her clit to the other side of her hips and begin slamming her down on me. The tightness from the contractions has set me off, and I refuse to hold it any longer. I begin cumming inside of her, my head swirling from the orgasm. With every thrust, torrent after torrent shoots into her, and she rocks back onto me to ensure she gets every drop.

As my body finally stops having spasms, I fall onto her back and wrap my arms around her. She begins giggling as she starts moving back onto me again.

"Oh no, we can't again, I'm already late now!" I shout as I quickly pull out of her and begin scanning the floor for my clothes. She arches her back, looking back at me as I watch my own cum start to leak down across her clit.

"You sure?" she asks. I bite my lip hard and actually start considering it. *What is wrong with me?*

"No, I can't. I'm really sorry. Rain check?" I sigh as I pull up my trousers.

"Sure, since it rains nearly every day," she giggles and flips around, perching on the chair with her legs open, "Or I could just be here when you get back?"

"Sounds wonderful," I say as I make my way to the door. I need to get out of here before she pulls me in again.

"See you when you get back," I catch her wink as she bites her lip.

Okay, so now I look like shit and smell like pussy. Maybe the council won't notice. I mean, have those guys ever been introduced to a pussy in their lives? Probably not. Even if they had, they likely wouldn't remember.

I step out of my front door to a brisk breeze hitting my face. It is actually a relatively mild day; at our elevation, it is typically pretty windy. SkyWaard has always amazed me. Though some people in the community leave much to be desired, the city itself is immaculate. A work of art. A network of zeppelins in a cog formation anchored together by the council ship in the middle. Roads are paved with bronze and people are constantly zipping from place to place, their steam-powered automobiles fueled by water that has been collected from the condensation in the air. The entire city floats in place, constantly ascending and descending two inches, give or take.

SkyWaard is a place of art, of music. A place without war and a whole population working on the latest technology. A city where smiling faces are the norm, and no one ever complains.

That, in itself, is what I find so very irritating. People are not happy all the time, so why do we put on this charade?

I begin walking on the bronzed path and pass a few people wearing their three-piece suits with their decorative accessories. I have my own accessories, of course. My favorite I built when I was fifteen years old and have modified and improved upon it throughout the years. It looks much like a common bronze bracer, but acts not only as a watch, but as a weapon and shield. From firing spring propelled bolts, to a hatch that rolls out tiny mines, this thing has gotten me out of countless less-than-favorable circumstances. It is my pride and joy.

I move casually over the walkway towards the council ship, where I am greeted by a rather large fellow with his arm jutting out to block my path. He looks to be guarding the place, perhaps, and is as intimidating as he is tall. His dark eyes seemed to stare right through me.

"Yes, hello. I am here to see the council; my name is Sebastian Lucas," I say, trying my best to sound proper.

"They are waiting for you inside. Do you have any weapons?" the man asks in a gravelly voice.

"No sir, just my watch and my suit," I lie. It's not that I intend on causing any trouble, I just hate parting with my baby.

"Head in, and keep your hands visible at all times," the guard grunts.

I pass the man, who never takes his eyes off of me, and open the double-doors. They are decorated with a large carving that represents the council, a circle encompassing a triangle. It is said to portray the three acting councilmen, working together as a unit. Some find great meaning in the symbol, but I've never been one for such foolish ideas.

I step into the dimly lit room, where a row of lights shine down on three elderly men. They all look haggard, like a lifetime of stress has manifested itself onto their faces. I suppose someone has to carry the burdens of those smiling fools who are constantly bumbling around SkyWaard.

"Approach," the old man in the middle croaks out, with his long, dark garb draped over his body – same as the others. I graciously move to the front of the room and I can't shake the feeling that I am being judged.

"Sorry I am late; I was... held up," I say to the men, hoping they are, at least, a little bit understanding.

"You will never be late again. We will not tolerate an act of insolence such as this in the future. If it happens again, we will have you locked away in the brig for treason," his angry response almost makes me flinch.

Guess understanding isn't their strong suit. Perhaps I should have brought Angelica with me to give them a visual understanding of what I was up against. I can hardly be blamed for taking the girl up on her offer; I practically deserve a medal for turning down round two!

"You know why you are here, correct, sir?" the man asks, his question brings me back from my wandering thoughts.

I clear my throat, "Yes, I do. I am to be an ambassador of sorts to the ground folk. To speak to them of trade?"

"Yes. You will be an extension of SkyWaard. What you do on the ground matters. I will be direct; we have chosen you because this is a small settlement and word of your charm travels – though I fail to see it today. Nevertheless, you and two others will be shuttled down tomorrow morning," the man says.

"May I ask, why are we considering trade with the primitives?"

"Mr. Lucas, have you not noticed that we are running out of room? Out of food? We need their resources on the ground just as they need our technology to move forward in the world and stop praying to fire or whatever idiocy they have grown accustomed to," his tone suggests the answer is obvious. Admittedly, it is, but I needed to be sure.

"I have noticed. So I am to set up a way for us to barter, using our technology as leverage in negotiations?" I ask rhetorically.

"Precisely," he says as he raises his hand in dismissal, "And, Mr. Lucas, please try and remember how important this outing is. This is not a vacation. You are there on behalf of everyone in SkyWaard. Try your best to stay out of trouble, and report back as soon as possible."

I flash the man my trademark grin, in a last-ditch effort to charm the old geezer, "Absolutely."

He does not look convinced.

Chapter Two

They say that you should love the place you're born and the people around you. That it's automatically ingrained into your soul, your being. For me, that couldn't be further from the truth. I am an outcast, just some nobody that our time cares nothing about.

This is why I do what I do. I take what they want to give me, I take on their memories, I take on their suffering and their pain, and I dispose of it. I don't provide this service out of the goodness of my heart – this is no altruistic act on my part, no. I do it for the money, for

23

the *power*. The power of knowing that they really don't want to come to me, but they have to… and they'll pay me for it. The simple fact is; they have no choice. I am one of a fucking kind.

"Loriella!" I hear my name being called from a distance and I whip my head around to try and locate the source. I crane my neck, peering through the people milling around to see if I can spot anyone I know. No luck.

I carry on, sloshing through the muddy ground. That's the one thing I truly hate about this place— the fucking mud. The rest, I don't mind. I can appreciate the sturdy stone walls that surround us, they keep us safe and protected from the forest goers. And I love the little thatched roofs on the wooden cottages that our people constructed all those years ago. So much history in those little buildings, it is a wonder that they have stood the test of time.

So, it isn't all bad here. But is it enough?
You hear a whisper that maybe there is
more beyond the walls of Ariviil; Sky
people that live far up in the clouds,
never coming down to ground. A city of
floating zeppelins with majestic and
lavish buildings, happy people and gilded
streets – all floating right above us.
Could it be true?

I suppose all that talk is irrelevant,
anyway. Just fanciful imaginings,
probably. And down here, we do okay.
We have the lumber mill that supports
many families by offering work.
Admittedly, that's one job I would hate;
to work in fear that the very delicate
truce we have with the forest people
could collapse if one-too-many trees
were taken from them. It's an incredibly
high-stress profession, when you take
that into account.

No, I'm quite happy to live within my
stone sanctuary. I have a home, I have a
job, and I even have a few close friends.
No family, not anymore. I won't talk

about them; it only darkens my mood. I can feel the tingling in my fingers, now, as the current feeds from the anger that is rising deep inside. I push thoughts of them deep down, locking them away where they belong. They're not worthy of having any of my emotions.

"Loriella, do you have a moment?" I hear a strange male voice calling my name. I turn around and the slight breeze whips at my hair as I bring my hand up to shield myself from the sunlight, trying to catch a glimpse of the man behind the voice.

"Derek," I smile when I finally recognize him, "What can I do for you on this beautiful morning?" I ask, a hint of sweetness to my voice.

"I need a fix, anything to make it go away, but I need more, it's not enough now," he begs, the words flooding out of his mouth in a desperate ramble.

I do feel sorry for him. Not too long ago, he lost his wife and kids to the conditions we live in. Life in Ariviil is not easy, by any means. We have to grow our own crops and hunt our own meat. Some people can't manage to fend for themselves. Others, well, they barely manage. When old age or sickness hits a household, it causes a weakness that few can overcome. Sickness weakened his family, and eventually claimed them.

"What do you want this time, Derek?" I ask. Last time, he asked me not to take all the memories away, he wanted to be punished for not providing for his family – for letting them perish while he still roams Ecta.

"Take it away, make me forget. I know you can. I want you to fuck it from my mind. I know you can! I have heard the stories," he pleads with me.

To look at, he is nothing special. He is wearing tan cloth pants and a white shirt with a fitted vest over the top. His features are plain and unremarkable, nothing that stands out. His scent isn't too pleasant; he reeks of the mud from the animals that are in the barn where he labors, the mud that clings when you walk through their filth. The aroma overpowers my senses the longer he is in my presence.

"Of course, Derek. Are you sure that you can do this, that my appearance is what you desire?" I ask him, trying to keep the retching from my voice.

"I know you can be whoever I want you to be. I want to fuck my wife one last time before you take her from me," he says.

I try to stem the tear that threatens to fall down my cheek; the emotion that is pouring from every ounce of his body is overwhelming. I feel everything he is giving off. It cloaks the air around me, making me breathe it all in, making me soak up every drop.

I grab a little vial from the table behind me, making sure I collect the one that will make him see what he wants. It is also something that will make him a little bit nicer for me. I can't take the smell much longer.

"Here," I hand over the vial, "Take this, and you will see what you want to see." I watch with rapt attention as he tentatively lifts the bottle to his lips, smelling it first. He will smell nothing but lavender; the ingredients to this particular brew will remain a mystery. A feature that not only makes the potion more appetizing, but also masks the ingredients.

I take special care to protect my recipes. I would be absolutely lost if anyone managed to get ahold of my book. The old leather binding contains pages full of spells and potions that I have created. Most of them, I can recall from memory, but there are a few special ones that aren't used so often in there, and I need the book to craft those. It's my pride and joy.

Finally, he tilts the vial back and swallows the drink whole. Within a minute, the potion will work and he will see me as whoever he wants me to be. His face morphs with relief as the potion takes hold, and I walk a little closer to him so that I can take him by the hand to the little room through the back.

"Faye? Oh, Faye… is it really you?" the look of sheer joy on his face halts me in my tracks. I can't speak, as the potion is only a mask. It persuades the brain to see what it wants to see. So, I just nod, watching him as he rushes towards me. His arms encircle me and his grip tightens around my waist.

He picks me up and pulls my body higher so that he can bring his mouth to mine. All I can smell is lavender as he kisses me hungrily, it's pouring from every cell of his body. I let him lead the kiss, feeding from his emotions I try to hold back the moan that threatens to escape my lips. He starts walking backwards, with me still wrapped in his arms. I don't

think he is going to make it to the
bedroom – the desire within him for his
dead wife is overpowering my senses.

I feel the thud of the wall against my
back as I am pressed against it. His
kisses move to my neck — not romantic,
feather-like kisses — hungry, desperate
ones. It only fuels my hunger more and I
shift my hands down, feeling his chest.
The months of not eating right have left
his body thin and boney. A pang of guilt
runs through me at the thought of him
not eating correctly. I push it down as I
move my hands lower to the belt that is
woven through his trousers. I make
quick work of the buckle, and due to his
weight loss, the trousers fall to his knees
with no effort from me.

My legs are draped around his waist and
his hands are roaming my body with a
hungry intent. I can feel it all — his
wants, his needs — controlling him,
pushing him to take me. The pain of
knowing that this will be the last time

that he ever spends with his wife is trying to claw its way to the surface.

I work his cock in my hand, feeling it harden even more under my touch. I push down with a steady grip, holding for a second before I move my hand back up, slightly grazing the tip with my thumb before I push back down again. He is moaning into my neck and his hips are jolting uncontrollably with each tentative movement of my hand. I bring my legs down from his hips and slide down the wall so that I am standing before him. His hands shake as they approach the belt that I'm wearing – it clasps the two sides of the dress together, keeping me covered. Underneath my attire is nothing, my pert chest and the slight swell of my hips are perfect for the mind to feast upon. It really wouldn't make sense to wear more than this when I see people, it would only make things harder for them. All they want to do is float away on a feeling of euphoria.

His hand traces the line of my body, sending a jolt of pleasure straight to my core. His hands creep lower, exploring my body, until his fingers find the little nub. He presses his fingers down and rubs in small circles, the motion sends a wave of moisture between my legs, preparing my body for the main event. He slips one finger inside, gently pushing it deeper, and my walls contract with the pleasure coursing through my system. I find his mouth and crush it with my own to prevent myself from moaning or crying out in pleasure.

It's an overload on the senses, my emotions mixed with his. They are making me climb that little bit faster. I don't need to feed him emotion at the moment, as he thinks I'm his wife. So, it's all there for the taking; love, lust, hunger. I want to take them all, because when he is finished, I will take his last memories of her. I will relieve him of this never-ending suffering.

I fall over the edge, moaning into his mouth as pleasure consumes me completely. As I come down from my high, he picks me up again and my legs automatically hook around his waist, his cock is sliding back and forth through my wetness, the head catching my clit and sending little sparks of pleasure to the tips of my toes. He pulls his hips back and forth, one last time, his crown placed at my entrance. One fluid push and he will be where he wants to be – well, he will think he is where he wants to be. At the end of the day, my body is just a vessel.

His hips bang against my thighs as he plants himself all the way inside, the movements jerky at first as he tries to find his rhythm. I grip onto his shoulders, urging him with my body to move faster, so he can find what he needs. His pace quickens and his thrusts grow stronger, I feel him hitting deep inside. His mouth latches onto my nipple as he keeps his pace, his tongue gently swirling around the hardened tip before he moves to the other to pay it equal attention. It works, I can feel the tightening of my muscles, my back straightens as I try to chase the wave, to feel it take over my body in an epitome of pleasure. This is where I need to be so that I can take his pain.

He grunts and his hips buck forward, I feel the warm jets firing deep within me, his cock pulsing as he finds his release. He cries out her name as his orgasm continues, and it's enough— that feeling of complete happiness and relief sends me over the edge. The bright lights that burst behind my closed eyelids tell me I am there; I am where I need to be. I kiss him one last time, deep and full of sorrow, draining every memory of his family from him. I know that when it stops, he will see me and smile, thinking he just fucked me. He will think that he is a free man, able to fuck who he likes, when he likes. He won't remember anything else.

True to form, he eventually comes around and leaves with a smile. Now, it's me that's a rumpled heap on the cold wooden floor.

My back arches as I try to absorb his pain. It's always the same, I can't control the aftermath. I ride through it all, every bit of heartache and pain. It's like reliving it through a dream, only I can *feel* everything. My heart beats faster, with every second I get closer to feeling her pass. The fever is taking over my body, I shake and convulse with every deepening feeling, waiting for my body to absorb the pain. Finally giving out, I drift off. The sleep will allow me to recover from the overload to my body and senses.

I awaken, cold and mostly naked, on the floor at the back of the room. My dress is open at the front, leaving me feeling exposed. I pull my dress around me when I sit up, replacing the clasp before pulling myself up to stand. I feel a warm trickle down the inside of my thighs.

Making my way to the other side of my room, I put some of the water from the bucket into the large pot to wash myself.

It's bloody freezing! There is no way *that* is going anywhere near my foo. I feel the tips of my fingers heating up and the air charges around me. I place my hands on either side of the pot, knowing it will only take a few seconds to heat the water a little.

After I wash and sort myself out, I make my way back over to my workspace, ready to make myself a little something to stop any little ones from making an appearance. Everyone loves the idea of family – kids surrounding us, laughter echoing out all around us – but that's not for me. I won't be adding to the population any time soon. I have too much to offer to be stuck raising a child on my own from one of my little encounters.

I have trinkets and potions lining the shelves, the bare wood walls are comforting and homey. For me, the simple furniture scattered around the room creates a feeling of warmth and welcoming, it entices people to stay when they come through the door.

The best part of the room is the glass mirror I have. To walk in you would think it is a normal mirror, but alas, no.

This mirror helps you see a version of yourself that you love. The effect does its job well and people want me to offer more of that perfect illusion, to take what they see and help make it happen in real life.

I can't plant a whole new way of life into their minds, but what I can do is take the bad memories, the painful ones, and erase them through touch. Whether that is the touch of a hand, or the caress of skin, or the act of a kiss. My favorite is through sex, that ultimate bliss. I can take them, too, with some of my potions. I use them to absorb their emotions and feed them what they need. They escape for a moment, and when they leave, they leave the memories that plagued them.

The back is where the magic happens, my old wooden bench is where I am happiest. I am at home amongst the glass vials with brightly colored liquids, taking in all the different aromas that drift through the air and wrap around me like a blanket. This spot just has everything I need to create, I feel at ease with my herbs and salts. The smells that emanate from different combinations of ingredients soothe me; this is happiness for me.

I quickly down the vial of potion that I've concocted that will prevent me from becoming pregnant. It doesn't taste the best, but it does the job and takes the possibility away. Thankfully, I don't have to take it every time, it lasts for a little while before it wears off.

As I glance around my table, I am reminded that I need to gather up some more ingredients. The money I got from

Derek will go a long way to buying what I need. I have a couple of new things I really want to try. I'm excited at the thought of experimenting, getting lost in the rhythm of my mind, working out what can be mixed together, what elements I can use to aid the creation of uniqueness.

I change quickly into my green cloth trousers, threading the belt around my waist and securing it. The belt holds one or two little potions in case I ever need them. Never forgetting it, I sheath my little dagger at the side, just in case. The brown leather corset I wear hugs my breasts without showing them off completely, whoever looks me over has to use their imagination as to what lies underneath. I am not huge, but I'm firm and high...

What's that saying? More than a handful's a waste.

The straps encase my shoulder blades, making my neck seem longer. I leave my hair loose, falling around my shoulders in soft caramel waves with what looks like gold flecks shimmering between the strands. I fasten the dark cloak around my neck and bring up the hood, my green eyes are illuminated all that more because of the depth of my cloak. I grab the satchel off the table and make my way out of the door, making sure it's locked behind me.

Let's see what the little village of Ariviil has in store for me today. I wonder what new adventures may be lying in wait, or if the town will be exactly how it's supposed to be, how it always has been – a stone imprisonment, made to shelter and isolate.

Just once in my life, I want to be able to feel the unexpected.

Chapter Three

The air is unusually chilly at the docks and the cold sends a shiver down my spine. The cold or the anxiety, either or. This will be my first time away from SkyWaard, and though I am truly excited to embark on this journey, I can't help but feel uneasy about the challenges that face me on the ground below.

The transportation shuttles are made of brass and are harnessed by a large parachute made of cotton. No propulsion here – only have enough fuel to get me back, in fact. Should something go wrong... well, I'll be a sitting duck.

"Come now, I haven't all day," I say, using my most urgent tone.

The man carrying my luggage gives me a look of contempt as he delicately places my gear into the shuttle, and by delicately I mean he slams them in with no regard for my personal belongings. "Good riddance," the sturdy fellow grunts as he passes by me.

I decide to be the bigger man and simply walk away. Sure, I could probably have him locked away for his snarky behavior, but what is the point, really? No one can ruin my day. I won't give him the satisfaction.

I step into my shuttle. Of course, the thing is about as spacious as a can of tuna, but it will do for the short trip down. It will have to; it's not like I was given a choice in the mode of transportation. I wish I were given a choice, perhaps then I wouldn't be worried about the grease stains never coming out of my suit.

The lid to the shuttle snaps shut as a giant steel claw positions itself overhead. I lay back and look through the glass port on the side as the claw comes down and clasps around the shuttle. I suddenly feel my stomach flip as the machine starts to lift me into the air.

Feelings of nausea take over my body once the machine comes to a halt. The swinging sensation that follows does nothing to quell my fickle stomach. A loud alarm sounds and the claw releases the shuttle. A surge of adrenaline courses through me as I am sent careening towards the ground.

The feeling is amazing; I have never felt such a rush. All the chemicals I have dumped into my body over the years, and nothing has ever made me feel this alive. It's like my mind is swimming inside my skull!

The sensation is abruptly stopped as the parachute flies out and my fall slows dramatically. I slowly start to feel my weight come back to me. My smile is wiped from my face as the rush and the adrenaline dissipates.

As I hang in the air, I begin to wonder how I should present myself to the people below. What are their customs? Does one shake their hand like in normalized society, or something else entirely? These people could still be worshipping fire for all I know, or for anyone knows, really. We have tried our very best to keep our exposure to the primitives limited.

I don't have long to dwell on it; the shuttle comes to a stop quickly. The landing was softer than I had anticipated. As the door slides open, I am consumed by a world of green and gray, along with the stares of about a dozen men encroaching on my personal space.

Their world is beautiful and the architecture is fascinating. I see huge stone walls off in the distance, huts built from a strange material I have never seen before, and people in absolutely strange garb.

The women are hardly dressed! They won't hear any complaints from me, but how do they even stay warm?

I step out of the shuttle and take in the sights and scents around me. The food smells incredible. This world is so different than the one I am used to, such a contrast from the smells of metal and oil. There is life down here, a whole ecosystem full of biodiversity. I am captivated.

"Are you lost, friend?" a woman's voice is heard in the distance.

I turn to see a stunning woman with golden colored hair and a light complexion. She is curvy and seems very aware of it as she walks towards me, lightly swaying her hips. I almost lose my manners and forget to look at her face, but common decency pulls my attention back up to meet her beautiful green eyes. I am a gentleman, after all.

"I am lost, actually. Can you help me find the nearest wine establishment?" I ask. The woman walks within an inch of me, barely leaving me room to breathe without my skin pressing against hers.

"Wine? I've never heard of it. We have lager and bitter, though, if that's what tickles your fancy."

Her voice… That accent… It's like their words just roll off of their tongue effortlessly. Makes me wonder what else they can do with their tongues.

"Sure, that sounds great. Lead the way?" I say back as I grab my luggage. The girl gives me a peculiar look as she sees me pick up my belongings. The same type of look any outsider gets.

She begins leading me through a crowd of men, all nearly twice my size and clearly unhappy to see me. Or untrusting of me, I'm not really sure. Does it matter? These guys could hurt me very easily if they wanted to. Good thing I keep my wrist device on me at all times. It does a great many things, of which can include murder, should the need arise.

"At this establishment, are there beds? Dining?" I ask.

"Yes, we have beds…" she says, trailing off in bewilderment at my ignorance.

I really hope I haven't offended her. Nothing wrong with being thorough, right?

As we walk into the hut, the light from candle flames dances against the walls, illuminating the room. I may have misjudged the place, actually. The abundancy of food they have lining the tables would make even the highborns in my ward jealous. The more I see from these people, the less I think we have to offer.

Two men approach quickly, relieving me of my luggage as the woman grabs my hand and leads me to a table. I can't help but have an odd feeling in the pit of my stomach, but I am willing to overlook it at the prospect of booze. Something is off about this place, but perhaps the ale will numb me enough to ignore it.

"I feel terribly embarrassed, but I haven't asked your name," I say as I sit down.

"My name is Jemma. Yourself?"

"Sebastian."

"Well, nice to meet you Sebastian. Are you hungry?"

Yeah, but I was hoping to taste you. "Famished. What's on the menu?" I say, trying to conceal my smirk.

"Menu? There is no menu. Just what we have in stock. Today we have boar, ale, and cheese. It will have to do."

"Very well, then. Seems you have it all worked out," I say, letting my eyes wander down to her cleavage.

I get a good look before bringing my eyes back up to meet hers. A smile forms across her face when she realizes what I was doing. I can feel warmth spread across my cheeks and realize I am now blushing; even more damning evidence that I am a pervert. Great.

The two men who took my luggage reemerge with massive plates of food. I'm not sure what was wrong with the food already laid out, but they sure know how to make a guy feel special here. They set the plates down and Jemma waves them away.

"So where do you come from, Sebastian?" she asks, sliding over a chunk of meat.

"I came from a place called SkyWaard. I am actually here to speak to someone in charge of your settlement. Perhaps negotiate trade, if possible."

51

"Oh, you will want to speak to Mia, and the rest of the elders. They live in the center of the city, in the Temple District."

"That information was very helpful, thank you," I say with a smile.

Jemma stands up from her side of the table and begins walking seductively over to me. Once she reaches me, she sits down next to me and places her hand on my thigh.

"Well, I have fed you, sheltered you, and given you everything you've wanted. Now, are you ready to return the favor?" she asks as she lets her tongue pass over her bottom lip.

Seems I have the same effect on women down here, as well. The men standing by the exit give me cause for concern, but who am I to question their customs? "Okay, name your favor, Jemma," I say, trying to act innocent.

"I think I would rather show you," she says as she once again rises from her seat, this time leading me with her.

The heat that was once in my cheeks begins to roam across my body. The hair on my skin stands as she leads me past a doorway. I only catch a glimpse of what's inside, but it appears to be an array of bottles and plants of some sort. The room itself is nothing special, but the energy flowing from it is almost divine. I would have stopped and explored, had it not been for the gentle tug on my sleeve leading me to another room.

As we cross into the designated room, Jemma pushes me back onto her fur-covered bed. I land with the elegance of a drunken dock worker, then look up to see her removing the only bit of fabric on her body leaving anything to the imagination. Once her straps are removed, her perky tits bounce into place and she begins slowly crawling up my legs, careful to let her nipples graze across my skin.

"I think I know the favor now," I say with a grin as she moves up my chest, brushing her breasts against me and she places her index finger on my lips, urging me to shut up.

I comply completely, and Jemma gives me a devilish smile before she begins kissing down my chest, careful to keep her finger in place. I can feel myself getting hard against the fabric of my pants, and I know she does, too. My skin feels as if it is on fire as she traces around my right nipple with her tongue before working her free hand into pants. She grips my cock tightly and slides her hand along the shaft, careful to avoid the head.

I want to give back, you know? Really help the girl out, but she has me completely immobilized. It's almost as if some sort of sorcery is at play. I have never been so turned on in my entire life. Could it just be these women? The way they dress? The way they talk and move? There is something nurturing about her... Something unfamiliar.

I begin thrusting my hips lightly, trying to meet her hand halfway, but she simply places her hand on my chest as if it is a warning of some sort. Her fiery eyes are locked into place and I can't pull away. I almost jump out of my skin as she brings her face back down over my nipple and gives it a few flicks. My hand is locked in her hair but she doesn't seem to mind, she frees herself from my grip with ease and glides down my stomach. In a flash she has my cock out, with a look of admiration on her face.

She gives me a brief smile before letting my cock pass through her lips, all while maintaining eye contact. My back begins to spasm and a swirl of euphoria swells up inside of me, I'm dangerously close to cumming and that would be a disaster. How could I look their elders in the eye after such a lackluster performance?

I try to think of something else; I even close my eyes and try to visualize something mundane, but I'm pulled back into reality with a jolt every time her lips pass over the head of my cock. She begins swirling her tongue around the head while her hand firmly grips the base of my shaft. She is winning this war and there is nothing I can do.

Her free hand moves up her own body and she slowly caresses her left tit as she continues sucking, picking up speed and suction with each blow. I can feel my cock beginning to jerk and know I'm right on the edge. I close my eyes in shame as I feel precum leaking out against her tongue, but then she suddenly stops.

I look down to see her smiling with her hand still on my cock, but now she moves her other hand from her perfect tits and starts caressing my balls. It's like she knew my absolute limit and met me head on. She's giving me a recharge. *Is she just toying with me?*

"How about I do something for you?" I say with my breathing ragged.

"Oh, you are doing something for me, Sebastian," she says as she squeezes the base of my shaft hard and slides her hand upward, pulling all of the precum out.

As I watch the clear liquid ooze out of my cock, she traces the underside of it, collecting all of the fluid. I watch in sheer curiosity while she brings her two fingers between her legs and guides them in. I find the act bizarre, but at the same time completely arousing.

She crawls back up my body, but this time I know the drill; I just let her take control. She brings herself back down onto my cock and slowly works her way back to my balls.

As my head passes through the ridges inside her, I feel her muscles stretching from the girth of my cock. Once she has the full length inside, she begins rocking on it, letting her clit slide over the smooth skin right above the base.

She lets out a moan as I bring both of my hands to the soft skin of her ass and give it a nice squeeze, guiding her down harder onto me.

"Fuck me harder, Sebastian..." she says, her voice trailing off.

Oh, now it's MY turn?

I begin slamming her down onto me as I work myself up to a sitting position. She throws her arms around my neck and buries her face in my chest and I use her own weight to bounce her onto me. As my cock slides in and out of her, she begins moaning loudly and clawing my back.

I pull her face up with both hands and make her meet my gaze just like she did with me before. She starts biting her bottom lip and trying to pull away, but I won't let her.

She is mine now, and this is payback.

I wrap my hands around her cheeks, interlocking my fingers behind her head. She can't escape now, not even if she wanted to. I start to feel her muscles contracting around my shaft as her legs start to shake. I can feel the urgency in her movements, the longing to cum. I was just in the same predicament.

She brings both hands up and moves her fingers through my hair, digging her fingernails in my scalp. Her eyes begin to gloss over and her pussy begins tightening around me wildly as she lets out a loud moan. I meet her moan with my tongue, feeling the vibrations pass through me.

I can't control it anymore; a flood of cum begins shooting out of my cock with so much force I'm surprised she didn't fall off of me. I moan involuntarily and pull her shoulders down, forcing her onto me even harder. As she rides the waves of her orgasm, she rocks onto me, working out every drop I have to give. We both collapse under the power of our mutual orgasm and her head falls flat on my chest.

The next thing I hear is a light giggle as she moves her finger up and down the center of my chest, smiling into my skin.

"That was amazing..." I say, panting without giving it much thought.

"If everyone fucks like you up there, please take me with you when you go back," she says, breathing heavily.

"After that, what's the point in going back?" I ask jokingly as I sit up in bed.

She smiles at me and starts putting her clothes back on.

"I don't suppose you have a restroom?" I ask.

"Go back out to the main room, then it's along the far wall."

"Perfect."

I finish getting dressed and walk out of the room with a triumphant grin. I follow her directions, but I pass by the same door I did before. I peek inside and see row after row of bottles and plants on shelves bolted to the walls.

Little peek won't hurt, right?

I step inside the room and feel that strange energy again. The hairs on my arms stand up and I shudder as I move deeper into the room.

"What are you doing?" a voice calls out.

I turn and see the most beautiful woman I have ever laid eyes on. She stops me in my tracks. I can't even speak. She has big green eyes, a hue of green I've never seen before on a person. They are entrancing.

"Well?" she says.

I can't make a sound. I can't move. My mouth is slightly open and I can't shut it. I try speaking, but only nonsense comes out. She smiles and begins laughing softly as she shakes her head.

"Cat got your tongue?"

Chapter Four

I inspect the fine man in front of me who is wearing a rather amusing look across his handsome face, and even more amusing attire. I wonder what has him so stunned, and what kind of place he might've come from that dresses their men up so strangely.

I have never seen clothes that look so odd. I notice his long, dark pants are pristine, not a single mark on them. My eyes trail across his body, taking in the white shirt that's neatly buttoned up to the top. There is something tied around his neck that leads down the front of the shirt, and he's also wearing a cloak of some sort, though I have never seen one so short and fitted. *Strange.*

As I look the man over, my pulse accelerates. I don't know a thing about him, and I may not understand his clothing, but one thing I do know is that he is setting my body on fire. I wonder if he is feeling a similar spark, so I try to reach out to draw his emotions in.

I can't feel him. It's the most peculiar thing, as if there is a cloud of black surrounding him and blocking me out. I can see him standing right in front of me, but I can't draw anything from him. My eyes ping straight back to his face and I know my stunned expression matches his, now. I have never experienced this; I've never been unable to feel someone.

Why now? Am I ill? Or is this strange man in front of me the cause? Whatever it may be, I need to find the answer. My livelihood depends on this skill of mine. I cannot lose it.

I realize we have been staring at one another for an uncomfortable length of time without speaking. "Hey!" I repeat myself, "Cat got your tongue?" I rest a hand on my hip and cock an eyebrow. He shakes his head, then seems to snap out of whatever trance he is in.

"What are you?" he says to me. I frown, that was not the greeting I expected. And what sort of a fucking question is that, anyway?

"What the fuck do you mean? What the fuck do I look like? I'm a woman, you arsehole!" I fire back at him. *How dare he!* No simple hello, no explanation as to why he barged into my quarters... just an incredibly rude question.

He recoils, clearly taken aback by my angry response. An apologetic expression washes over his features, "I'm sorry, you're right. I don't know what I am saying. I'm afraid you caught me off guard, that is all. Please, allow me to start over," he clears his throat, "Hello, I'm Sebastian. And you are?"

Wow. His voice is effortlessly captivating, the tones and the way he punctuates his words is an addicting sound. It's soothing and refined, like how some of the elders speak. It sends a jolt of awareness right through me, resonating on a deeper level than I have ever felt before. It's as if his voice is calling to my soul.

"I'm Loriella... And thank you for introducing yourself, but that still doesn't tell me why you're here in my quarters," I give him a pointed look.

Sebastian furrows his brow as if he is lost in thought, "I'm afraid I can't answer that. I'm not sure why I was drawn to this room," he offers a charming smile, "Perhaps that explains this whole cat-and-tongue situation."

"You're not from around these parts, are you? What are you doing here in Ariviil?" I ask him. I would've kicked any other intruder out by now, but for some inexplicable reason, I can't do it to this one. I have this overwhelming need to carry on talking to him, a compulsion I can't seem to shake.

"I see you are rather observant. You are correct in your assumption; I am not from the area. I'm actually here on some important business, and I need to speak to your elders. Do you know of anyone who might be able to facilitate that?" his cocky smile and arrogant charm are like a magnet, drawing me closer. No one around here speaks with such power; his words wrap around my body, making me hungry for him.

"I can take you?" I chirp. *What the fuck is wrong with me?* have clients that will need seeing to, I don't have time to be this man's guide.

He begins a slow pace around the room, his expression shifting from intrigue to wonder as he processes everything around him. It's understandable, my collection of ingredients is quite impressive. He starts snooping around the vials that are lined up along the walls, carefully taking lids off and smelling them.

"Would you, now? That would be very kind of you. And what, pray tell, might I have to do in return for this generosity?" his eyes glitter with mischief as he looks at me.

I attempt to hide the wicked smile that forms at my mouth, I don't want to reveal what I would *really* like him to do to me. I start to wonder if I can draw from him during sex. Perhaps heightened emotions would clear the fog surrounding him that keeps blocking me out? He seems like he'd give me a good ride, if nothing else, but I decide against it... for now.

"Nothing. I will take you to the elders, show you around a little, that's all," I shrug, "Although, I might have some questions about where you come from. By the way, where is that exactly?" I ask him where he is from again, not bothering to hide the excitement in my voice. We don't receive outsiders around here very often, and none have ever looked the way he does.

"I appreciate it. Lead the way, Loriella," is all he says to me.

I grab my cloak and satchel from the table and make my way outside, glancing back to see if he is following. When I look back, I catch his eyes roaming over my body. I turn forward and smile to myself. At least there is one person who wants my body, not just an illusion of somebody else.

Outside, the pungent air hits me hard. I trudge through the sludge, making my way towards the market. If I'm taking him to the elders in Temple Heights, then we're going to walk the scenic route. I did offer to show him around, after all.

Truthfully, I want to spend as much time in his presence as I can. I can only feel my own emotions when I am with him, it's actually somewhat of a relief. My mind travels back to my instantaneous need for him; I can't push it out of my mind. I want a chance to explore every part of his delectable body.

Picturing him in my mind as I continue walking, I start to think about the way his shoulders fill out that funny looking cloak. He is not huge by any means, but he has an athletic build. Tall, lean and powerful. My mind travels to darker places... I want to see what lies beneath that odd attire. I want to lick every inch of him, savor his taste. If he tastes anything like how he smells, he will be delicious.

I shake the thoughts away and glance back again. Sebastian is wearing a look of sheer contempt as he tries to avoid the filth of the streets. I want to tell him it's no use here, filthy straw and mud perpetually line our walkways, there's just no way around it all. I watch his eyes scan the surrounding buildings as he takes in the city and I wish I could get a read on him, just a quick glimpse of what he feels about our little safe haven... or what he feels about me.

"So, tell me about where you're from," I smile, trying to distract him from the grime. The way he's carefully placing each step is pointless. He might as well forget about keeping his shoes clean.

"SkyWaard," is all he says, as he points to the clouds above.

No, it can't be. Surely, it's only a myth? Is he teasing me? We've heard stories of the people living in the sky, but in hundreds of years we have never seen one of them. Looking at him, I realize that it's possible... and surely that would explain his unusual clothing. I wonder if this is why I can't read him, perhaps the people of the sky have their own magic that counteracts ours? I need to know more; my curiosity is piqued now. I need to find out everything I can from this Sebastian of SkyWaard.

"Really, now? You are serious? I've heard a few stories, but I've never actually met anybody from SkyWaard. What's it like to walk on the clouds" I ask him with childlike enthusiasm as adrenaline spikes through my body, sending that familiar spark to the tips. The magic and the raw emotion combined is a heady mix.

I see his eyes fly down to my hands when he notices the magic that's trying to leave my body. With all these emotions running through me, I'm having a hard time keeping it contained.

"What's happening to your hands?" he frowns, a concerned expression on his face.

"My magic," I say in explanation, not even considering that he might not know what that is. When I see the look of disbelief on his face, I know this to be true. I continue in an attempt to explain, "I possess the power of elemental magic, so I can manipulate fire and water. Sometimes, it flares up a bit when I get too emotional. It's inconvenient at times, but it really does help with what I do for a living..." I quickly cover my mouth, realizing my mistake. I shouldn't have said that. Now he is going to ask me what I do, and when I tell him he is going to look at me like I'm some kind of freak, just like they always do. The pang of despair hits my gut like a punch, taking the breath from my lungs.

"Are you alright?" he asks me, his voice filled with concern.

I can't catch my breath quick enough to answer, so I just nod at him.

After a few seconds, I manage to calm the emotional storm that is coursing through me. Straightening myself upright, I prepare for the questions that I know are coming. It's human curiosity; we have to know everything about the people we are connected to. I just don't want to see that inevitable look of disgust on his face when he finds out what I do.

"So what is it that you do?" he tilts his head. *And there it is.* I knew it was coming. An innocent enough question for most people, I suppose. I can't blame him for not knowing the pain it causes.

Maybe this is for the best, I reason. If this has to end, then I would rather it end right now. I don't think I could handle being with him longer, trying to hide it from, only for him to find out later. And then I'd see what I always see on the face of everyone who has ever claimed to love me as soon as they learn of my gift. *Disgust.*

"Well, I suppose you could say I help people... with potions and such," I say hesitantly.

"You're being very vague, Lori. I'm going to have to insist on more. How can we understand your land if we don't know anything about it?" his voice holds that hypnotic tone that makes me want to tell him everything he wants to know. A smile tugs at my lips, I like that fact that he shortened my name of his own accord. The few girls who do talk to me call me that, but I prefer the way it sounds coming out of his mouth.

"I create potions, and healing tonics and such. I take people's pain awa—" I start to explain, but he interrupts me before I can finish.

"I'm interested in the 'and such' part. How else do you take the pain away?" his brow furrows in curiosity. Damn, he's perceptive.

"By touch. I can make them feel what they want to feel, and I can remove their memories by touch. The more contact, the greater my strength…" I don't go on. I can't. How else can I say it without spelling it out for him?

"Are you saying you can take other people's emotions… and project on to them what you want them to feel?" he sounds fascinated.

I nod at his summary and watch him carefully, bracing myself for the typical reaction. It doesn't come, though. Instead of radiating disgust, he appears thoughtful. Calculating, even.

"Well now this trip to the Temple just became a little more interesting," he smiles as we pick up the pace, heading through the bustling streets to get to our destination.

"I think you were just about to tell me what it's like to live in the clouds," I say after a moment, trying to change the subject. Besides, I really am curious. I can't imagine how it would work. He doesn't seem to have any familiarity with magic, so I assume that is probably not how they do it. Trained birds, then? I wrinkle my nose at the thought of the mess that would leave on the ground. Probably not that, either.

"We live on zeppelins," he answers quickly, "They hold our buildings and streets up, high in the sky. Buildings of such grandeur, nothing like you have ever seen before. It's a captivating city, everything is gleaming brass and polished stone..." his voice trails off. He seems very fond of SkyWaard, very proud of his home. After a moment, he continues, "You see this watch that I'm wearing?" he sticks out his arm so I can see, "I made it myself. Adapted it to become a shield, and other things, should the need ever arise."

I think my chin must be touching my chest, my mouth is hanging open in shock at the thought of such a thing. It shouldn't be possible! Nothing could keep buildings that heavy up in the sky. *Could it*? I want to ask more, but we're not too far from our destination. Wandering through the encircled fortress doesn't take long, even when taking the long route.

"I must admit, everything here is quite different than what I expected. You seem to have everything you need, and more. Food, shelter, warmth..." his last words spoken have his eyes drifting down, locking on the little honey pot that most men want to taste.

I feel myself blush as his stare lingers a little too long. *Shit! I need to get myself under control or I'm going to end up telling him to fuck me already! Why does this man do such things to me?* I look away from him and focus on the trail ahead of us while I regain my composure.

The pathways get better as we near our destination, but the sixty-four steps that we need to climb to get to the temple are awful. I don't understand it, having the elders at the top of all these tiresome stairs. I suspect they put the temple there for the sake of their own self-worth, a symbol of superiority; a way of telling the commoners down below that the elders rule on high.

As we start up the stairs, I realize that I have not been back here for a couple of years. And then, another thought stops my heart; I can't believe it didn't cross my mind before now. What if I run into my father? What will I say? I didn't even consider it before agreeing to take Sebastian here. This is what happens when I let my emotions rule over my head.

My father is one of the elders. I try to fight the rage that begins to boil at the thought of him. I will not be a welcomed sight, walking into the temple. I am an outcast here, I was turned out because I am different. They don't understand what's different, they don't even try to understand what is different; they refuse to accept it, and they hate it. When the elders found out what I could do, they convened a meeting and made my father choose between his place with them, or me. He chose them.

Since that day, I have been on my own, trying to find my own path in this god-forsaken world. It's hard when people don't understand; when they judge without compassion. It took me months to get a decent home to call my own. I was living on the streets, doing whatever I could to raise enough money to get myself a place to sleep. So many times, I went hungry because I couldn't afford to eat. Time slowly moved forward, and eventually I found a way to use my empathy to my advantage, finally securing an income and a place to lay my head.

"Not much farther now, it's just up these steps. Through the main door, you will see the elders," I tell him, hoping he can't detect the distress in my tone.

"Alright, Lori. Thank you for bringing me here. The journey has been pleasant up to now," he sounds optimistic, "The people I've encountered have been so hospitable. If this is any indication of your people, I trust this meeting with your elders will go quite well."

I snigger at his comment. He hasn't seen anything yet. The common people might be somewhat pleasant, but the elders are a class all of their own. They are the ones you have to watch out for; they do nothing unless it means a gain for themselves. They see hungry people; they don't offer food. They see a child without a family; they don't offer shelter. It's terrible, but that's the way it's always been. And to think I used to be part of it!

"It was my pleasure," I say before my curiosity is gets the better of me, "You never did say why you wanted to talk to them…"

"Ah, right. Well, it is an important and somewhat delicate matter. To start a dialogue and open up trade between our communities. To see if we can unite again."

My eyes widen as he tells me this ambitious plan of his. I don't have the heart to tell him to keep his expectations low. Really, I wish his plan were possible, but our communities are completely different entities with such a strong divide between how we operate. I don't think the elders are going to take to kindly to this. Unless, of course, there is something in it for them. Maybe Sebastian has more up his sleeve than he is letting on?

We reach the top of the steps and look up at the huge, wooden double-doors that are directly in front of us. I don't want him to see me hesitate—after all, he thinks that we are one great big happy family—so I continue forward without missing a beat. Who am I to spoil his illusion? In a matter of minutes, he will manage that all on his own.

I push open the door to reveal the interior of the temple and we walk inside. The solid wooden floors are the first thing you notice when you walk in; the rich darkness of the wood makes it seem so welcoming, even if it's anything but.

"This place is impressive," Sebastian says to me.

"Yeah, it is," I sigh, "All of the elders and their families live in this castle. They employ some of the common people to do the housekeeping, cooking, and other odd jobs around the place," I glance around for a moment, then turn to him with a tight smile, "Right, it's just through these doors. Would you like me to wait outside so I can guide you back to the village, or do you wish me to leave?" I smile to hide my frustration as I try to draw from him again. It really is getting to me that I don't know what he is feeling, it's like navigating a darkened room. I can't stand that I feel so unprepared when I speak to him, that I have no way of sensing his true emotions. It is a dangerous thing, to flirt with the unknown. I know this, but I can't walk away. I'm incapable of fighting this allure that he has.

"No, come inside with me," he doesn't ask, he demands, which excites me in a way. He has me under his spell, I know I should be running as fast as I can away from those doors, but I can't bring myself to leave.

"Okay," I squeak out before pushing the door to the grand hall open. I know the elders will all be sitting inside, perched around a table as they wait for anyone brave or foolish enough to try to talk to them. Every day, the elders do this. It always seemed rather boring to me, but I suppose that's a small price to pay for status and power.

As we step inside, my eyes quickly slide across to where I know my father will be stationed. I smile inwardly as my eyes catch his expression. The look on his face is priceless, he's clearly shocked to see his own daughter is the one who brought the man from the sky to see the elders.

I smile a full, beaming smile, knowing that I have just rocked the boat even more.

"Elders, I would like to introduce you to Sebastian, from SkyWaard."

Chapter Five

"A pleasure to meet you all. Let's get to business, shall we?" I say, smiling at the two men and the very attractive woman in the middle.

"Excuse me?" the elderly looking man on the right croaked out with a look of disgust on his face.

"Oh my, where are my manners? I am Sebastian Lucas of SkyWaard. I come bearing a proposal for you and your fine city," I say with an exaggerated bow.

"Do you dare come in our chambers and demand our attention? Furthermore, what is with your clothes? Did you dress yourself, or are you drunk?" the man replied.

"Well, I had a little help getting dressed, and hungover is hardly the same as drunk," I smile to the man who is growing redder by the moment.

"Excuse our fellow council member, he seems to forget that he does not speak for all of us. I am willing to hear you out, but first I will have to ask you to have your friend wait outside. We do not like her kind in our chambers," the middle aged man on the left said.

I look back at Loriella, then back to the council.

"She stays," I say without a second thought.

The women in the middle finally looks up from her podium for the first time and smiles, "Very interesting. We have not seen the people from SkyWaard for hundreds of years, and yet here you are; at our doorstep and demanding an audience. Do you defy your elders where you come from, Sebastian?"

"No, but where I come from, when a guest brings another guest, the host doesn't try to split up the party," I say.

"Fascinating. Very well, your friend can stay, but know that her presence will bear weight on our conversation. Our community is built on reputation, and hers is quite a burden to tack onto your name," she says, twirling a quill between her fingers.

"Nothing to fret over, my back is strong enough for the both of us," I say with confidence.

"Carry on, then," the woman says, shifting her dark brown eyes across my body.

"I am here on behalf of my council, we wish to once again open trade with your settlement."

"You canceled trade with us hundreds of years ago and disappeared into the sky. Your people refused us trade or access to any of the wonders that keep your fortress afloat, and now you want our help?" she says, licking her soft pink lips.

"That is the gist of it, yes," I say, scratching my head.

"What would we get in return for such an outrageous request?"

"We would share our technology with you. We would send people down to educate you, we would show you the wonders of the steam engine. Imagine it; no need for horses. There's so little upkeep for your transportation when you don't have to feed and shelter it. We can also give you access to our propulsion technology, allowing you to move from one place to another in almost an instant!" I say, excitement building in my voice.

"If you're offering all that, then you must be desperate. Let me guess, since you spent so much time in the sky, you have run out of food?" she asks, smiling.

"Along with other valuable resources, yes," I say with a straight face.

"So, what is stopping me from letting you all dig your own grave? We have been getting along just fine without your help for centuries, and now you come to us for aid? Why would we want the technology you have, if it can't even keep your people alive?" she leans forward on her elbows.

"I admit, our council was a bit shortsighted in their act to cut off all trade, but please don't let the mistakes of our forefathers punish our children today," I plead.

"Maybe we can work out something. An arrangement of sorts…" she says, trailing off as she rises from her chair to expose a slender, yet curvy, frame.

"What do you propose?" I rise to my feet as well.

"Meet me in my chambers, we have much to discuss." She says as she turns to walk away.

The two men to either side of her appear to be angered, but they do not utter a single word. I now know who is really in charge, here.

I turn to Loriella and mouth the word "Sorry."

Loriella wears a look of disgust and dread on her face. I can tell by her expression that she knows something I don't about this woman. I'll need to ask her about that after the meeting.

I follow the woman past the two men – staring me down much like the first group I encountered at my landing – and into her chamber. As I cross into the room, candlelight flickers across the floor and I see the silhouette of the elder woman standing over by the window, masked by moonlight.

"Well, here I am, speak," I take a seat in the wooden chair that was prepared for me before I stepped in.

"Your lack of respect… while I find it irritating, I also find it somewhat… erotic," she says as she pulls another chair just inches from mine and takes a seat.

"Well, I suppose a thank you is in order?" I smile, "I apologize, I don't know what is customary here for compliments."

"That's right, you do not know our customs well, do you?" she asks as she puts both of her hands on my knees.

"I do not, no," I shake my head. Their customs are very strange indeed. In SkyWaard, if a girl touches your legs like that, it means she is hoping to find her way between them.

"Well, in situations like these, it is considered proper to seal these deals with a fuck," she says, sliding down her gown.

I guess some things aren't so different.

As her gown falls onto the chair beneath her, the candlelight dances against her body and I catch short glimpses of the perfection that it really is. I find myself wondering why they are called elders to begin with, she can't be over thirty. Her body is exciting; she is short with small, supple tits. Her hourglass figure comes out at the hips, making it increasingly harder to look away.

"All of your transactions are done this way?" I ask with a puzzled look.

"Not all, just the important ones. Unless your name is Loriella, of course," she hisses as her hands travel up my thighs.

"What do you mean by that?" I ask as I place my hands on hers, halting their movement.

"Oh, she hasn't told you? She fucks people for money. She calls it 'taking their pain away', but the rest of us call it 'being a whore'," she sneers, resuming her ascent up my thighs.

"Are whores looked favorably upon down here? In SkyWaard, it is a profession claimed by the lowest of class," I say, disconcerted by this new revelation.

"It is the exact same here. Now, enough talking. Do you want this arrangement to happen, or not?" she says as she brings her face within a centimeter of mine.

Well, it is their custom, right?

I put my hand around the back of her neck and pull her in tightly, locking my lips with hers and letting my tongue move past her lips. She presses back, matching my own intensity and begins moving her tongue against mine. The sensation of the soft flesh intertwining sends a rush of blood to my cock.

I pull away for a moment at the realization that I don't know this woman's name. It's not the first time this has ever happened to me, but she seems rather important.

"I'm really sorry for this, but what do I call you?"

"My name is Mia, and don't be sorry, I never told you. That's my fault," she says, sliding her hands into my trousers and massaging my cock.

I run my hands up her sides; her skin is so soft to the touch. I stare into her dark brown eyes as she nibbles lightly on my lower lip. Her dark hair flowing down her shoulders is perfectly straight and almost majestic.

I brush her hair aside and move my hand up to softly cup her pert tit as she climbs on top of me. I use my free hand to work my trousers down as Mia offers no support, wiggling in place and making it even harder.

Once my pants are out of the way, she grips my cock hard in her hand and guides it into her tight warm pussy. A sudden thunderbolt of exhilaration courses through me as she places her hands on my shoulders for leverage and rocks slowly on top of me.

Wetness forms on the front of my fabric as her clit swipes it with every lunge into me. She never breaks eye contact, not even for a moment, and it drives me absolutely crazy. I try to look away, but she pulls my chin back to the front, never letting my attention falter.

Everything from her scent, to her own brand of allure pulls me in. I'm hooked. She moves her body like a serpent and her breathing increases with her movements. Every hiss that passes by my ears makes me crave her even more.

I place my hands on her hips and help guide her, lifting her entire weight with every lunge, ensuring that the entire length works in and out of her. She presses her forehead to mine, keeping her gaze locked in and I can't help but wonder what sort of magic she brings to the table.

As her pussy tightens around me, I feel my legs begin to shake beneath her. The glimmer and mischief in her eye lets me know she's onto me and can feel every twitch inside of her.

I am now at her mercy, a pile of putty beneath her and she is using her body to mold me. She hooks her legs into the arms of the chair and begins grinding me harder, giving me no relief. I can tell that she is getting off to the knowledge that I am helpless.

As she writhes against me, I bring my face down, careful not to break eye contact, and begin moving my tongue around the rim of her darkened nipples. I feel them tighten as my breath and tongue make contact and she lets out a tiny moan.

With her body pressing against mine and the sensations flowing through me, I ignore all pain. The fatigue I would normally feel over this kind of exertion is gone and I squeeze her tit as I form a seal around her nipple with my lips.

I moan into her breast as I feel the urge to cum building inside me. Mia grabs my face with both hands and pulls it up to lock our gaze once more as my cock swells inside of her.

I can no longer take it, and with her body making contact a few more times, I explode inside of her. Bliss washes over my entire body and I feel myself jerk wildly inside of her as multiple spurts leave me. Mia breaks our gaze and begins kissing me deeply, sucking my tongue as I continue to cum inside of her.

In a huff, I finally finish, and Mia pulls away, smiling.

"How was that?" she asks as she climbs off of me and grabs her gown.

"The most fun I have ever had securing a trade agreement," I laugh, smiling as I pull up my trousers and stand.

"Well, I have considered the agreement... and I have to say, Sebastian, I'm going to pass," she said flatly.

"Pass? What do you mean pass?" I ask, completely confused.

"Pass, as in, I changed my mind," she says with a cold tone.

"No... you can't do this. People are starving up there!" I say as the anger inside of me begins to build.

"I can do whatever I want, actually," she shrugs, pouring herself a drink of wine, "Your people had no issue with abandoning our kind when we were starving. Why should we care if you starve, now?"

"What are you talking about?" I frown.

"Oh, that's right. You don't know the truth, do you?" she raises the glass to her lips and takes a sip before continuing, "Not only did your people leave and isolate themselves away from Ariviil, they also took with them our food, all of our reserves... they left behind an entire civilization of people. They abandoned us to starve, no one on the ground should've survived with the meager crops we had. We did, though. We learned, we provided for ourselves, and we persevered... despite the ruthless actions of SkyWaard. Well, now it is our turn to be ruthless. Not only is it a 'no', it is an 'absolutely never'."

"This will cause a war!" I scream.

"If it's a war you want, then we are more than happy to provide one. You can't even feed your soldiers; how do you expect to do battle? Foolish boy," her tone is condescending.

I begin panicking. If she doesn't agree to this deal, we are *all* done for, including them. The council will not just *let them win.*

"I can't let you do this. I'm so sorry..." I say as I aim my wrist towards her chest.

"What are you going to do with that puny thing?" she asks with a snicker.

I fire a small electrified harpoon into her chest, instantly immobilizing her as she falls to the ground. I can hear her breathing, but she is now unconscious.

Fuck! What do I do now?

I straighten my clothes and walk casually out of her chamber. The guards by the door continue looking straight ahead and do not seem too suspicious.

So far, so good.

I walk around the podium stands where the elders convene to see Loriella still waiting for me. I make my way over to her and quickly grab her arm.

"Come with me, we have to leave now," I say nervously.

The two guards by the door disappear into the room I just exited from.

"Wait, what did they say? Have they agreed to the trade? Where is elder Mia?" Loriella asks.

"Seriously, we don't have the time for this, my dear," I say as I tug her away.

The guards reemerge from the room with a frantic expression on their faces.

"YOU TWO, STOP!" one of them shouts.

"Loriella, I'm so sorry," I say as I put my wrist to her head.

"Sebastian, what are you doing?" she asks in a confused tone.

"I panicked in there. Your elder didn't keep her end of the bargain."

"Stay calm," Loriella says, pulling a potion out of her bag.

The two guards conjure fire in their hands and take aim at us. Loriella tosses back the potion, and the expressions of the guards immediately change.

"Don't fire on them!" the older of the elders' shouts.

What?

I begin walking backwards with Loriella until my back presses against the big wooden doors. The guards to the side open the doors for us and I turn my back to the room. As we walk out into the street, all of the guards lower their weapons and clear a path for us.

"What is happening right now? Why aren't they firing on me?" I ask.

"I need to concentrate. Just keep moving, Sebastian."

We walk for a while until we finally reach my shuttle. The guards stay close, but refuse to raise their weapons. I climb inside the shuttle before pulling Loriella on top of me. Once she is cleared, the door slams shut.

"Hold on tight," I say as I push the big red button in the center.

Loriella grips my thighs as the shuttle blasts off and shakes the ground around it. Through the port on the side, I can see people scattering as they become small specks on the ground.

"Why didn't they attack me, Loriella? What was that?" I ask as we break through the clouds.

"The potion increases my power and reach. They all saw me as the person they love, or want the most. Why? What did you see me as?" she asks.

"I just saw you..."

Chapter Six

He just saw me.

At least I know he wants me, then. I still draw a blank when it comes to pulling emotions from Sebastian, so this new bit of information is an interesting development.

I look outside the shuttle. The clouds break, and I see a world that is beyond comparison to anything I have ever known. I'm stunned into silence; how is any of this real? As we hurtle towards it, I'm absolutely mesmerized. I see stone everywhere, peeking through the clouds as we near the city in the sky.

The brass interwoven with stone is truly a stunning sight to behold. As we get closer, the details get better. I notice a huge clock tower. The stone tower opens up and right at the top you can see the gears of the clock, enormous wheels of metal steadily turning in reliable perfection. As the gears turn, you can see the hands slowly moving around. It's fascinating to watch.

I turn my head and my eyes scan the other buildings. It all looks refined and crisp, there isn't an ounce of dirt anywhere to be seen. I look down at my attire and I suddenly feel out of place. Now I know how Sebastian must've felt when he first arrived in Ariviil.

"Hold on, my dear, this is going to be a bumpy ride!" his tone is ever charming. Even in the midst of peril, Sebastian doesn't lose his charisma.

I grip the seat as hard as I can, holding on with everything I have. It's then that I realize I can do more than just sit here. I can try to smooth the ride out a little.

"I can help, Sebastian," I say, "Let me put a shield around the ship to ease the landing." My voice is confident, though internally I'm freaking out. I have only ever successfully managed this technique once... and that was only around myself. I was avoiding someone else's fire and it just happened through pure instinct, my hands dove to my satchel to retrieve what I needed and the incantation poured from my lips without a second thought.

"I don't see how your talents as a whore will be of any use to us right now, but thank you for the offer," Sebastian sneers. I recoil; where did *that* come from? His cruel words are like a blade right to the chest. I knew that this would happen once he found out; that he would see me like everyone else.

"Yeah, you're probably right!" I snap as anger blankets the hurt. "And please! You couldn't pay me enough to suck your cock, let alone fuck you," I say to him venomously, I want the words to hurt as much as he just hurt me.

I can't even get the satisfaction of knowing that they did. All I have to go on at the moment is the look on his face, the way his eyes turn cold. His muscles bunch with tension, he seems ridged with coiled up anger just trying to break free. He bottles it, though. He has to remain in control because if he loses it, we won't be walking away from this alive.

I grip the seat harder and draw my legs up to my chest trying to protect as much of my body as I possibly can, hoping and praying that our landing goes smoother than I'm imagining.

His skill is masterful as he steers the ship into the dock, and I let out a relieved breath when the shuttle lands without incident. The docks here are totally different than the ones we have down below; our wooden structures with stone posts to tie off ships are simple and primitive compared to this. I realize it's just simplicity made grand; SkyWaard emphasizes aesthetics and appearances are a priority. Down in Ariviil, functionality is the only thing of real concern when it comes to architecture.

I drink in everything I possibly can with my eyes; it's like peering into a dream. Two pillars of lights illuminate the paved ground where you step off the shuttle. I notice the docks have wide openings to accommodate different sized ships, and there is a border of intricate brass railings along the paths to stop you from falling over the edge.

Everything is really hovering in the sky.

I move from my seat, no longer content with just peering out of the window. I want off this shuttle; I want to explore.

"Come on," Sebastian says with a gruff command to his tone. I follow him to the door of the shuttle and prepare to step out into the unknown. "Stay close to me."

I don't question his words, I just simply grip his hand tightly and follow him. His words from before still wound, but what else can I do? I don't know where I am or where I would go without him to guide me.

I can't help but take in the beauty of this place as we cut through the city. The different colored buildings grab my attention; magnificent structures that seem to never stop climbing, constructed of stone that varies from white to red.

I notice the people walking around. The women are stunning, wearing dresses that cling to every curve of their bodies, their assets pouring over the top of the tight corsets. They wear silly hair styles that seem to make them seem taller, and their legs can clearly be seen, as if on display to entice. Even the men look dapper. They all are dressed a lot like Sebastian, but with different accessories. Some are in very tall hats, others have lenses attached with tiny chains to their odd fitted capes, and some even wear what seem like goggles covering both eyes.

To say that I feel like the odd one out is an understatement.

I finally find my voice, "Where are we going?"

"We're going to my place, for now. I need to prepare to see the council tomorrow. We need to tell them that your people won't cooperate," he frowns, lowering his voice so others don't overhear, "This is going to cause all-out war. SkyWaard cannot sustain and we need Ariviil's help to survive. Your people refused to cooperate freely, and I can't see the council taking that news very well. If diplomacy fails, they will force cooperation through violence. They have no choice but to let our entire civilization starve, otherwise. How are we ever to live in a world of peace and evolve if they refuse to work together?"

I try to absorb what he's saying as he pulls me through the doors of a stunning building. The sashed windows that lead up even higher into the sky catch my eye and instantly my heart beats faster. What would it be like to live in a world with gizmos and gadgets around every corner, to have all this technology at my fingertips? Mix all this in with a few of my spells, and I could pretty much achieve anything I wanted. The thought of playing even more with the elements and combining them with a manmade force intrigues me.

We walk through the lobby of his building, I feel so out of place. Looking down at what I'm wearing, my downtrodden clothes are an eyesore. The disapproving stares people cast in my direction aren't out of the ordinary for me, I'm used to being looked at like an outcast. At least I'm used to it, it doesn't sting so bad this time around.

He hits the button on the wall and I hear the clunk of gears and the screeching of metal against metal. As it gets closer, the sound reverberates through me. The swipe of the doors as they part for us to enter brings me back to a feeling of pure elation, this is something else I have never experienced before.

I take a tentative step inside, testing my weight, then continue into the box once I feel it is safe. I walk closer to the darkened wall, near the brass hand rail that runs around 3 sides of the small, tomb-like box. I take a hold with my free hand, gripping tightly. The doors close, encasing us completely inside with nowhere to go. Anxiety builds in my body and I glance at Sebastian. He seems calm, so I can only assume it is normal for this box thing to trap people.

I flinch as the box starts to move. The rumbling beneath my feet, the flutters in the pit of my stomach are all new emotions that are firing every cylinder in my body. The metal conducts the power in my hands and sparks emerge from my fingertips, flying all around the lift. I watch as Sebastian ducks to avoid the oncoming onslaught. It's just nerves finding an outlet; the sparks won't harm him, but he doesn't know that.

"What the—" he puts his hands up to shield himself, "Loriella! What is wrong with you?!" he sounds frustrated. "Do you want to draw attention to us?"

As if I did it on purpose.

"Get yourself under control," he hisses, straightening his fitted cape once the sparks calm down. "I know that you're

111

probably craving attention, since I pulled you away from your townsmen who regularly provide it, but we have more important things to deal with right now and we need to keep a low profile until I've worked through a plan."

I push down my temper, holding it all in. I'll wait until we are behind closed doors, then I am going to let it rip. He hasn't seen anything, yet.

The box stills, then opens to a large open space with a couple of closed doors along the perimeter. The detail on the doors is remarkable; ornate latches and intricately designed handles. The doors have little glass holes to peer through, but as we near them, I notice that the glass changes color and I can't see through it.

He unlocks his door and opens it, gesturing for me to follow. I step inside to something majestic, it's simply out of this world. Every minute detail is polished and refined and classy. It shows he has wealth beyond anything I could ever compare with. Everything seems to have a strategic place, his expensive furniture is positioned for maximum effect; the room is both welcoming and intimidating in its splendor.

I stop in the middle of the large room, bracing for the argument that is sure to happen. It pains me that this is even happening, but I need to know how we got in this mess, and I am sure he has questions since he now knows the full truth.

"What will you tell your council?" I break the deafening silence that has formed between us. Sebastian walks closer and stands right in front of me. His body towers over mine, so I tilt my head up to meet his gaze. I stop short and the breath leaves my body as I momentarily lose myself in his commanding blue eyes.

"I will tell them the truth; that your people will not help us. They are deceitful and do not honor their word. They casually dismiss the lives of an entire populace of people without a second thought," his voice never wavers as he speaks, and that irks me even more.

"What do you mean by deceitful? You met a handful of people and you try to paint them all with the same brush?!" I say, my voice raising slightly though I keep myself calm. Well, for now, anyway.

"Every person I met in that place was deceitful! You lied, Mia lied, Jemma... well, I don't actually know that she lied, but I assume that's simply because I didn't talk to her long enough to catch her in one. My point is, how can our societies forge a symbiotic relationship when one of those civilizations uses nothing but manipulation to get what they want? There can never be trust, and trust is essential for peace."

I'm stunned. What am I supposed to say to that? I have no account for my actions, as I did lie... well, I misled. That's different, right?

I deflect, "How did elder Mia lie? She just took you to her chambers to discuss your business, how is that lying? She heard you out and gave you an answer, I'm sorry if you didn't agree with her decision but that isn't deception, Sebastian."

It's then that it all comes flashing back, the pieces start coming together; the elder laying on the floor of her chambers, the guards chasing after us, rushing into the shuttle to flee to the world above.

"What happened to the elder, Sebastian?" I question him, worry seeping through my anger. His eyes look sorry for a split second, then as quick as it came, it disappears.

"You want to know what happened?" he sounds angry at first, then his tone turns regretful, "Of course you want to know what happened. I did pull you along with me into this mess, didn't I, Lori?" he sighs. "Fine, I will tell you. When we went to her chambers, she seemed onboard with the trade negotiations. We had a customary fuck to seal the deal, then after she got what she wanted, she backed out of it. She made sure to drive the knife in, as far as you're concerned," the volume intensifies with each word that leaves his sensual lips. He reins in his anger as he finishes his explanation, "I panicked and shot her in the chest. It only immobilized her, just something to buy us some time. She's still alive, just probably a smidge angry with me, I'd imagine."

He fucked Mia? I don't think I can get past that. *And what is he talking about, 'customary fuck?'*

"What do you mean, she talked about me? Is that why you were saying all of those cruel things to me? She told you I'm a whore, didn't she?" I demand an answer, my tone leaving no choice. "And you *fucked* her? You thought it was a custom? What do you think my people are, feral animals?! That's horseshit, Sebastian, and you know it! You need to take some responsibility, here. You went around thinking with your dick, instead of your mind. Instead of acting in the interest of your people, you chose to do what made you feel good in that moment, and look where it got you!"

My body is on fire as I hold his stare; I'm burning from the inside out. I can't control it. I can't push it back down. I'm brimming with a mixture of anger, lust, and need. The need to consume, to feel, to be wanted is riding me hard. I can't help it; it's not often someone wants me as I am. I'm so angry with him, but his words from before are still there, holding me hostage.

"I only saw you..."

Even though I can't feel his emotions, my potions should still work on him... so that must mean he wants me, right? I'm confused, the way he looks at me now; he wears that same disgust that everyone does when they find out what I do. How can he want me, yet be so repulsed by me?

"I *was* thinking of my people! I wanted to find a workable solution for everyone, and I thought I had it. I wasn't going to just stomp all over the customs of your people and ruin any chance at cooperation by denying her! How was I supposed to know she was lying? Everything about your people is foreign to me, I was a fish out of water!" he shouts, "And how can *you*, of all people, judge *me*?! You fuck people for money! At least I was fucking one person for the sake of an entire civilization, not an entire civilization for a crust of bread—"

I don't let him finish, I bring my hand up so quick he doesn't even see it. I slap him across the face and the sound reverberates through the room, I use the energy that is coiled in my hands and send him flailing through the air.

"YOU KNOW NOTHING ABOUT ME!" I scream at him as he lands against the wall, falling to the floor with a thud. "You think you know who I am? Or what I'm capable of? You haven't got a clue! You're so backwards in your thinking that you can't see the wood for the trees! I could bring your world crashing down around you, I could destroy everyone you hold close to you, make them feel like their world is ending and there is no other solution but to give up on their sad excuse for a life. This bubble that you live in is not real, Sebastian! But I'm real, and you don't want to make an enemy of me, because I will wipe you from existence!" I watch his face for a reaction to my words.

He just smirks at me. *He fucking smirks*! It only fuels me; I walk closer to him and crouch down to his level so that I can wipe that smirk of his pretty little face.

"Alright, Loriella... It seems I do have quite a bit to learn about you, yet. Please, enlighten me on how you fuck people for money, but are not a whore," his eyes harden, but his disarming smirk is still there as he pulls himself up.

"I don't just take people's money and fuck them... it's only very rarely that I do that. How do I explain this?" I sigh, "Can you imagine losing someone you love, the person you care about most in the world, to hunger? To disease? Then having to carry on living without them, reliving your failings as a provider or protector every day? I help people who are living that. When they touch me, I can erase the memories of their loved ones, or the feelings of shame, feelings of guilt... anything I want to remove, I can. And yes, the most permanent way I can do that is through sex. The combination of physical contact and heightened emotions allows me to do a more thorough scrubbing of their mind. It's not me they see, when I do that.

Remember that potion I used on the guards? That's the same one; it convinces the mind to tell them that they are with the ones they want the most. That's why the guards never came after us," I explain, my voice as calm as I can manage. It's difficult, because right now I'm still angry.

Sebastian's patronizing look has shifted to one of intrigue, "Let me get this straight... I can take one of your potions, fuck you, and you'll make all the bad stuff just... disappear?"

"Yes, I think," I whisper, feeling rather exposed as I wait for him to make his next move. "Although, I am not sure how it would work with you. I can't sense your emotions like I can with everybody else. That's why I was so taken with you..."

He appears thoughtful for a moment, then a mischievous smile creeps onto his face, "Interesting that you cannot sense me. Perhaps a bit of physical contact and heightened emotions will do the trick. What do you say, my dear? Shall we put your theory to the test?" His voice has taken on that deep, sensual tone, again. It wraps around me completely, making me unable to resist his charm.

Before I'm able to answer, there is a loud banging on the door. Sebastian frowns, looking to the door, then back to me, apparently weighing the best course of action. Does he answer the door and risk breaking the spell he has me under, or does he ignore the demanding knocks and have his way with me? He leans in, attempting the second option, but another insistent string of knocks rattles the door.

He lets out a frustrated breath and shakes his head, locking eyes with me, "This isn't over, Loriella; I will find out how much power you wield by the time the night is through."

I just nod at him. My voice seems to have left me, I can't form a single word as I watch him stride to the door.

"The council wants to see you tonight, Sebastian. You know where to go, so don't be late. 7PM, sharp," the voice is strange. I can tell he's trying to sound braver than he is, I sense his nerves as he speaks to Sebastian.

"It was arranged that I would meet with them tomorrow," Sebastian answers the man.

"They know you are back, and they know you have one of *them* with you. You know this is unacceptable. You will go tonight and you will meet with your council as they have demanded," the man doesn't give him time to respond, I see him turn and march back from the way he came.

I jump as the door slams shut.

"Well... fuck," he rakes a hand through his dark hair. His shoulders slump and I can see the worry threatening to take him. I slowly make my way towards him, every ounce of anger is gone at the thought of him suffering.

I wrap my arms around his neck and pull him down to me, letting out a quiet moan as his lips meet mine for the first time. I can feel everything; the way his mouth molds to my lips to make me obey his silent commands, the way his arms wrap around my body to pull me into him, the way his hard body presses against mine with raw need.

For the first time in my life, it's only my own pleasure that I feel, and it is exhilarating.

His hands swoop down to my ass. Cupping the cheeks, he lifts me up and strides across the room to the sofa. Placing me down, he gently lays on top of me, his mouth never leaving mine. His hands make quick work of his clothes and before I even have time to register that he is naked, he is pulling and tugging at mine, hurriedly working to remove them.

I place my hands on his body, tracing my fingers along his defined abs and chest. His muscles are lean and sexy, not huge and overbearing. He is strong, it's as if power radiates off him in waves. I can't help but let my hands feast on every inch of him; I want to devour him completely.

I'm naked, beneath him on the sofa, and looking up at him as he takes in my body. His eyes trace me up and down and it sends a warm heat between my legs. I return the favor, scanning my eyes over his body again.

I see the slight patch of dark hair, the cock that points perfectly towards me, itching to be inside me. My eyes linger on the swell of the head, the ridge – I just want to see if it tastes as silky as it looks. I consider giving in to my curiosity, but before I have the chance his mouth latches onto the tight bud and starts licking and nipping.

My hips automatically thrust upwards in reaction to his onslaught. I moan, letting him know just how much I like his mouth on my body. His fingers wander down to my core, tracing the seam of my entrance, manipulating my body to do as he wants it to. I'm helpless to disobey. I feel myself getting wetter with every strum of his fingers until he finally grants me what I need, slowly pushing one finger inside and curling it forward, finding that spot and gently caressing it. I can't take much more; my body is wound so tight.

I'm not feeling anyone else's emotions; this is all me... with that thought, I explode around his finger. He slips it out, and as I ride the wave of pleasure, I feel him nudge me with his cock. I shimmy my hips closer, needing to feel all of him buried inside of me.

I'm not disappointed as he finally thrusts all the way inside in one swoop. As he pumps in and out of me, he surrounds every part of me. I feel him everywhere; his lips kissing my skin, his hands gripping my hips as he powers deeper with every thrust.

"Harder," I moan, hoping he understands me. I want him to unleash everything he has to offer.

His hips slap against my thighs as I pull them up higher, making him go even deeper. The glazed look in his eyes tells me he is right there with me, enjoying it as much as I am. His thrusting gets faster and harder as he pulls every ounce of pleasure he can from me. I feel the tension coiling inside me again, tighter this time. The tips of my fingers burn as his body drives me higher, and with one last punishing stroke, I fall over the edge.

My eyes roll back in my head and my toes curl. White spots cloud my vision as I reach that place where my power is held. I scream, my fingers claw down his back as I feel him coat my insides with every jerk of his hips. He stills and his eyes meet mine, a lazy smile adorns his stunning face as he pulls out of me gently and comes to lay beside me on the sofa.

As he pulls me into his embrace, I can't help but be in awe of what just happened. I never knew it would be like that. I never thought that my emotions, alone, would be enough to fuel something so intense. As I think on it, I begin to realize that it's not about the emotions of others; it's about mine, and how I feel.

That's what wields the most power.

Chapter Seven

The sun is finally setting on SkyWaard and I am no closer to finding the words I need to say to the council. My judgment is clouded by anger, though I'm not sure the source. Loriella had a life before me and couldn't have possibly had the foresight to know how her actions might affect me. Still, it's hard to shake, and I don't particularly know why. I can only assume one of her magic spells have worked and she is withholding that knowledge. I have never had jealousy or anything like it. So to be feeling it now, at her arrival? Too much of a coincidence I think.

A couple of hours have gone by since Loriella and I finished up, and we haven't spoken since. We are locked in a stalemate of silence, only glancing up to catch a mutual bit of awkward eye-contact here and there. The tension could be cut with a butter knife. Isn't sex supposed to alleviate that?

I look at my watch and see that there isn't a lot of time left before my meeting. If I don't make my appointment, they will come find me instead, and that kind of meeting I could do without.

"I'm sorry, love, but we must depart soon," I say, smiling to Loriella to mask any uneasiness in my voice. She looks at me from across the room with eyes that could pierce my heart.

"Yeah," she says as she straightens her rags.

A yeah? Is that all I'm worth now?

I feel a pang of hurt as I hear the disregard in her voice. The dismissal is almost too much to bear, and again, I find myself asking *why?*

"So, should we talk about what just happened?" I ask.

"Don't we have a meeting to attend?" she replies.

"Yes, but I thought maybe we could talk on the way," I say, trying to sound hopeful.

"Sebastian, there really isn't much to talk about. It was a momentary lapse in judgement. I know you don't respect me due to my job on the ground. Really, what is there to talk about?" she says making her way to the elevator.

"It's not that I don't respect you. It's just... I think perhaps our cultural difference is getting in the way here. You see, in SkyWaard, if you have sex with a lot of people, it reflects poorly on your character. I, of all people, should know and understand," I say with my eyes shifting towards the ground.

"So if you understand, why are you giving me such grief? I help people. In the end, isn't that why we all are here?" she asks.

"I completely understand why you do it, Loriella. Doesn't exactly make it any easier of a pill to swallow. In your culture, women are more free with their bodies, but up here it isn't that way. If you care about someone, then you have sex with only them," I say, becoming frustrated at the cultural barrier.

"Then do you not have sex with only one person?"

"I haven't found the one person I want to settle down with. Plus, up here, I'm a bit of an anomaly. That's why I said I can understand why you do it, but there is only room for one whore in this relationship," I say, smiling.

"You know, when you asked, I was honest with you. I feel something powerful for you, Sebastian. I wouldn't jeopardize that. We just met, but the connection I feel to you is unlike anything I have ever felt before. That is how I know it's real. This isn't some illusion of magic, or an attraction caused by some potion. This is genuine sentiment," she says as she grabs my hands.

"Loriella... I feel it, too, but our two worlds are about to go to war. I do not see my council reacting favorably to this news. With the best case scenario, even... how much further can this go?" I say with remorse.

"Do you think if I spoke to them, it would change the outcome? Perhaps I can use my gift?" she says, pleading with her eyes.

"No, you're not fucking the council, Loriella."

"No, idiot. I could use my magic to sway their opinions."

"I can't allow you to use your sorcery on them. They have to come to this decision on their own, free from influence. The council is wise, and this is the future of my people. I care about you, but this is the livelihood of everyone I have ever known. Even if you sway them against war, what then? Are we to starve? A whole civilization lost because of some petty grudge Mia holds with our forefathers?" I say as I pull Loriella into the elevator.

The elevator begins descending and I can see the grave concern on Loriella's face. I wish I could say something to put her at ease, but I'm a little on edge myself.

"So that's it, then? So many people are going to die... and for what?" she says.

"For the ignorance of the people in charge. Human history is littered with tales like these," I say, bringing both hands up to her arms and rubbing them lightly in an attempt to comfort her.

The elevator stops and the doors slide open. A small crowd of people are gathered around to spectate our walk to the council. It looks like news travels fast.

We begin walking at a brisk pace towards the central zeppelin that harbors the council, and what should be a quick journey is suddenly prolonged by a hoard of gawkers. Loriella seems uneasy and the crowd – while intrigued – show flares of anger.

Just how much do they know already?

As we approach the main doors, they suddenly swing open with two guards standing at either side of the door frame. We begin walking inside and the room lights up with the doors shutting behind us. The guards trail closely behind as we move to the central podium facing the council.

The entire council begins pouring out onto their podiums opposite of us, and none of them seem very pleased. With the men finally in position, the council members begin to speak.

"Sebastian, it has come to our attention that you have brought one of the Ariviilians to SkyWaard. You have risked the safety of our entire city, and I think we are all waiting on the edge of our seats to know why," the old man in the middle says.

"We ran into a minor incident and had to escape quickly, she helped me get here," I respond in the most respectful tone I can muster.

"Why then, did you not put her back into a shuttle and send her back?" the lines on his face deepen as his face contorts in bewilderment.

"I believe she holds valuable information, not only about the settlement, but about their leaders," I offer, hoping they listen.

Loriella appears hurt by this news, and I assume she thinks I am using her at this point, but it is a necessary evil. Right now would be a good time for her power to work on me, so she could see that I'm trying to keep her alive.

"You did all of this without our blessing, Sebastian. This will not go unpunished," he says.

"I understand. I would like to ask one favor, however," I say.

"You directly disobey us, then ask for a favor?"

"Yes, it's a small one, out of common decency."

"Go on."

"I would like it if Loriella could return to her people unharmed. That way, we can show them that we are not the people they think we are," I plead.

"Oh? What type of people do they think we are?" he asks.

"The kind that ditched them when they needed us the most. The kind that left them to die. We need to show them that we are different from our forefathers."

"Based on what you say, I can assume they did not agree to help us?" he asks.

"No, they didn't. Their leaders are under the spell of a woman named Mia. She is deceitful and power hungry, in my opinion. I do not think she can be reasoned with," I say honestly.

"So, as long as she is in power, they will not work with us?" he asks.

"I do not believe so, no."

"You say that this girl you brought from the surface has knowledge of the inner workings of the council, and the settlement. Perhaps she can be of use to us after all..." the man appears thoughtful.

"What did you have in mind?"

"Well, you said that with Mia no longer in power, the rest of their leaders may be reasoned with. So, I will spare your girlfriend... but she will have to kill this Mia character."

Before I can respond, Loriella storms forward with electricity dancing on her fingertips. "I will *not* kill one of my own," she hisses.

"I apologize for her behavior, council," I say as I pull her to the side.

"I won't do it, Sebastian," she says to me, her voice frustrated and hurt.

"Loriella, they will kill you. You don't even like Mia! She is a liar, and what I would consider a traitor to your people. She does not represent you well," I try to reason with her.

"It does not matter if I like her or not, I will not kill an innocent person. Things are not that black and white," she says.

"We really don't have time for this, Sebastian. Either she does as she is told, or she can live out her final days in a cell," the councilman says, letting his impatience be known.

"Just give me a minute to talk to her, please," I plead before turning back to face Loriella.

"Sebastian, it looks like your people are no better than mine! They are unwilling to listen to reason!" she says as her eyes begin shifting wildly in intensity.

"Give them a chance, Lori. They are just afraid," I say as I grip her hands. The electricity coursing through them makes my skin tingle on contact.

Two guards burst through the door and run to the center of the room with magnetic railguns in hand. They appear to be completely panicked.

"Sirs, the people of Ariviil seem to be preparing for war. They have begun setting up war machines and fortifying their perimeter," a guard shouts.

"We are out of time then. Guards!" the man yells.

Two guards approach Loriella, causing her to quickly back away from me and the podium. The air in the room begins to shift dramatically as she stretches her arms out to the side.

"Get her under control, and get Sebastian's watch!" the councilman screams.

I immediately back away from another set of guards who are approaching me. The wind inside the room is kicking up, causing the others in the room to shield their faces.

"I will not be your prisoner!" Loriella shouts as she lifts a few inches off of her feet and hovers in the center of the room.

The guards each drop to a knee and take aim at her with their rifles. I'm not even sure she understands the deadly circumstances she faces, or what a rifle even does. I have to act quickly.

I grab a knob on my watch and yank hard, causing an explosion of small pellets to litter the room. As they make contact with the air, a gas is emitted from them. Loriella's manufactured wind carries the gas around the room and the men's heads start to fall.

"Sebastian, what did you do? I don't feel so good…" Loriella frowns at me as the wind stops and she falls from her position.

I hold my breath and dive under her, catching her before she hits the hard ground. As she and the men in the room go unconscious, I hoist her over my shoulder and dart out of the room and back into the fresh air.

Outside, a crowd has once again formed and they seem angry. I fall to the ground with the unconscious Loriella and gasp for air. A few of the men outside look into the room and see the entire council incapacitated.

"Traitor!" a man yells.

"No, it's not what it looks like!" I yell in my defense.

The crowd is forming a circle around Loriella and I when a loud, low-pitched noise fills the air. It is deafening. The men around me begin falling to their knees, clutching the sides of their head.

I seize the opportunity and bring myself to my feet once again and throw Loriella over my shoulder. I walk over to the railing that borders the walkway and peer over the side, looking down at Ariviil.

Machines rise up out of the water and make their way onto land, like massive mechanized beasts. They open their metallic mouths and breath fire onto the walls of Ariviil. The citizens of Ariviil begin firing their arrows and trebuchets back, but it doesn't seem to slow down the machines.

"The council was wrong! They are not planning an attack on us! They are planning a defense against whatever those are!" I scream as I point over the siding.

The remaining guards and men who are scattered about outside quickly regain their wits and rise to their feet. In a panic, everyone runs to the railing of the ships and looks over.

"He's right! Something is attacking the ground folk, along with our food supply!" a man shouts from the crowd. I look over just in time to see that the councilman has regained consciousness and is walking at a brisk pace towards me.

"Arrest that man!" he yells to a guard, who doesn't seem to hear him.

I walk towards the councilman, meeting him halfway, "A new threat has appeared, sir. You can arrest me and Loriella if you wish, but while you waste time locking us up, our crops will be burning to the ground. I don't know what will come next, but I know one thing for certain. You will need me, and you will

141

need Loriella. So, what will it be, councilman?" I ask with a smug smile just as Loriella begins stirring in my arms.

Before I let the man respond, Loriella's eyes flutter open and she stares up at me in confusion.

"Sebastian, is that you?" she asks.

"Yes Loriella, it's me," I reply as I bring my hand up to stroke her hair.

"The council! Is everyone alright?" She asks with a hint of guilt in her voice.

"They're fine, and we are safe for now," I say glaring at the councilman.

"What do you mean, for now? What happened?"

"We're going to war," I whisper, turning my head back towards Ariviil.

Made in the USA
Charleston, SC
02 June 2016